Disney·PIXAR
MONSTERS, INC.

ADVANCE
PUBLISHERS

Published by Advance Publishers, L.C.
Maitland, FL 32751 USA
www.advancepublishers.com
Produced by Judy O Productions, Inc.
Designed by SunDried Penguin
© 2006 Disney Enterprises, Inc./Pixar Animation Studios
Monsters, Inc.
Printed in the United States of America

Sulley was Monsters, Inc.'s top Scarer and his best friend was his scare assistant, Mike Wazowski. In the city of Monstropolis, it was the job of the Scarers at Monsters, Inc. to collect the screams of human children by entering their world through closet doors. The children's screams provided the city's power. However, being a Scarer was a dangerous job. Monsters believed that children were toxic and it was deadly to touch them.

One day, Sulley and Mike arrived at Monsters, Inc. as usual. In the locker room, Mike and Sulley met Randall, a chameleon monster who was jealous of Sulley's status as top Scarer. He wanted to break Sulley's scare record. On their way to the Scare Floor, they passed Roz's office. She was the dispatcher in charge of Mike and Sulley's Scare Floor and always got angry with Mike for being late with his paperwork. "I'm watching you, Wazowski," she called out.

After a successful day on the Scare Floor collecting screams, Sulley stayed back to finish Mike's paperwork for him, so Mike wouldn't miss his date with his girlfriend, Celia. But when he noticed a closet door and went to investigate, a child followed him out! Sulley was terrified. Panicked, he shoved the kid into a duffel bag. But before he could get her back through her door, Randall came out and deactivated it.

Sulley took the child in the duffel bag to the restaurant Mike had taken Celia to. But before Mike had a chance to look in Sulley's bag, the kid escaped – and it was monster mayhem! Suddenly the CDA (Child Detection Agency) appeared and set about decontaminating the restaurant. Sulley and Mike grabbed the child and sneaked her back to their apartment.

Sulley and Mike tried to protect themselves from the child, but she liked the two monsters and even called Sulley "Kitty." As they got to know her better, Sulley began to realize that she wasn't really toxic at all, and nicknamed her Boo.

The next day, Sulley and Mike disguised Boo as a baby monster and sneaked her back to Monsters, Inc. But their first attempt to return Boo to her door failed and she wandered off. Sulley raced off to find her. Meanwhile, Randall realized what Mike and Sulley were up to and confronted Mike about Boo. Randall offered to help them out.

Mike and Sulley found Boo in a group of baby monsters. They grabbed her and raced back to the Scare Floor, where Randall had left her door for them. But Sulley didn't trust Randall. When Mike entered the door to show Sulley everything was safe, he was grabbed by Randall. Randall had been hiding inside, hoping to catch Boo, but he grabbed Mike instead! Sulley and Boo followed them to a secret lab, and found Mike strapped into Randall's Scream Extractor – a horrible machine meant to help Randall collect more screams.

Sulley rescued Mike and they ran to the training room to report Randall to Mr Waternoose, the head of Monsters, Inc. But when Waternoose saw Boo, he grabbed her! Then he pushed Sulley and Mike through a door. They were banished forever in the Himalayas with the Abominable Snowman! Mike told Sulley he'd ruined his life all because of a kid. Determined to rescue Boo, Sulley left on a sled to find a door in the local village and a way back to Monstropolis.

Sulley charged through a door and back into Monsters, Inc., and raced to Randall's secret lab where Boo was strapped into the Scream Extractor. "Kitty!" she cried as Sulley leaped to her rescue. Just then, Mike also arrived to help.

They ran back to the Scare Floor and Mike, Sulley and Boo went on a roller-coaster ride through the door vault, looking for Boo's door. Randall nearly caught up with them, but when he grabbed Boo, she fought back. She wasn't scared of Randall. Together, Mike, Sully and Boo pushed Randall through a door and destroyed it – so he could never return.

Soon after, the CDA arrested Mr Waternoose for trying to kidnap Boo, and Roz was revealed as a CDA agent, on undercover assignment to catch out Waternoose and Randall. She told Mike and Sulley that Boo had to go back to her own world. Sadly, Sulley said goodbye to Boo and she was led back through her closet door – then her door was shredded, so that no monster could ever scare her again.

Months later, Sulley was president of Monsters, Inc. He had learned from Boo that laughter was more powerful than screams. The Scare Floors were now Laugh Floors and children's laughter powered Monstropolis. One day, Mike told Sulley he had a surprise for him and led him to Boo's old door. He had reconstructed it. Sulley opened the door. "Kitty!"

The End